Sa
and the Elf

award

Saffy had a new home.

"I want to see the garden," Saffy said to Dad.

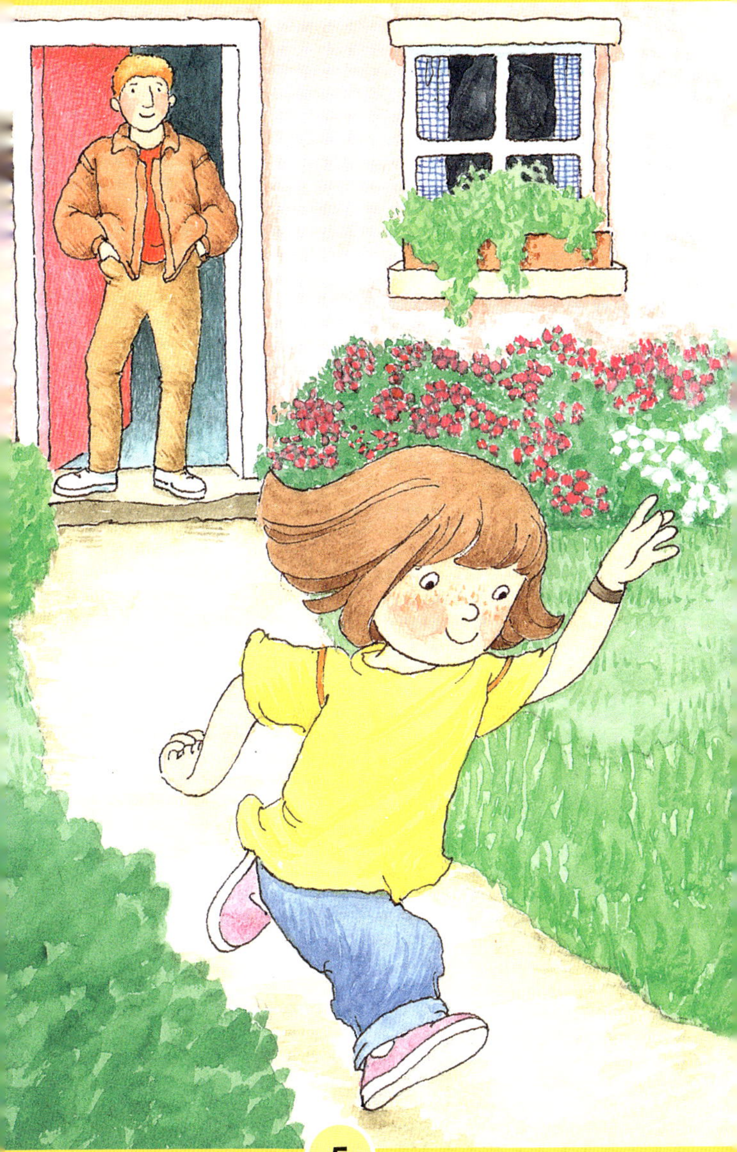

Saffy made a den
in the big garden.

Then she heard someone sobbing.

It was an elf. He was in a sad mood. The elf said, "I am so alone."

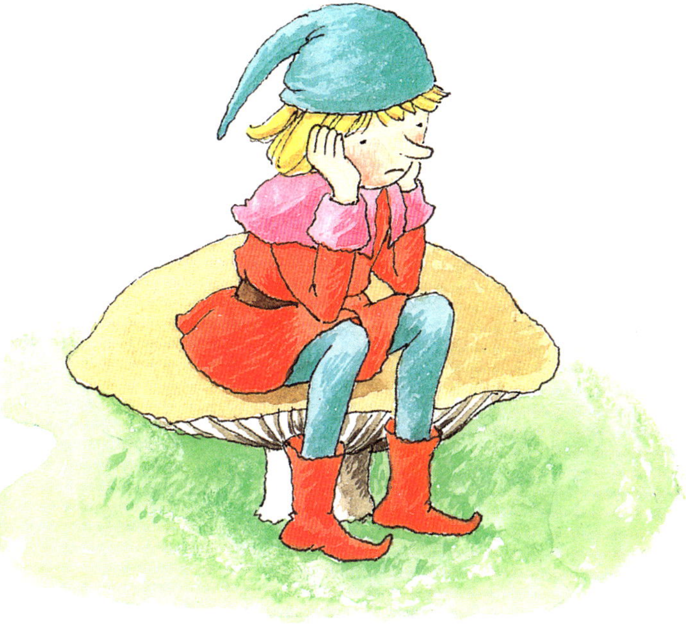

"Don't cry," said Saffy. "I will play with you. You will not be alone."

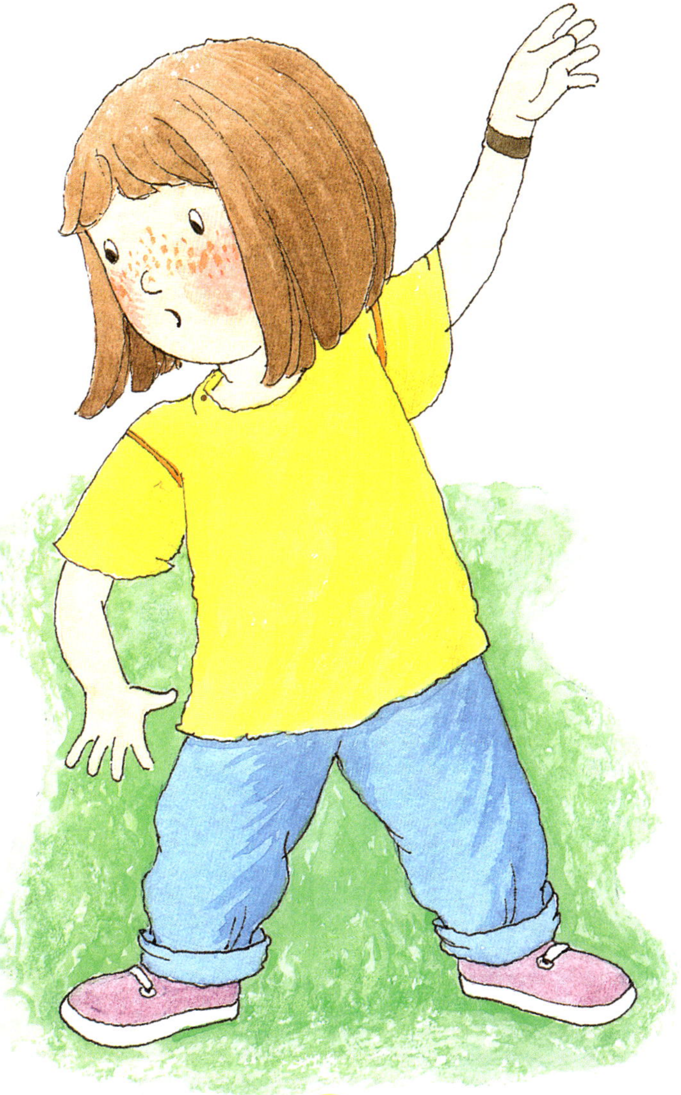

Saffy got her paints and tea set from the house.

"Have fun!" said Mum.

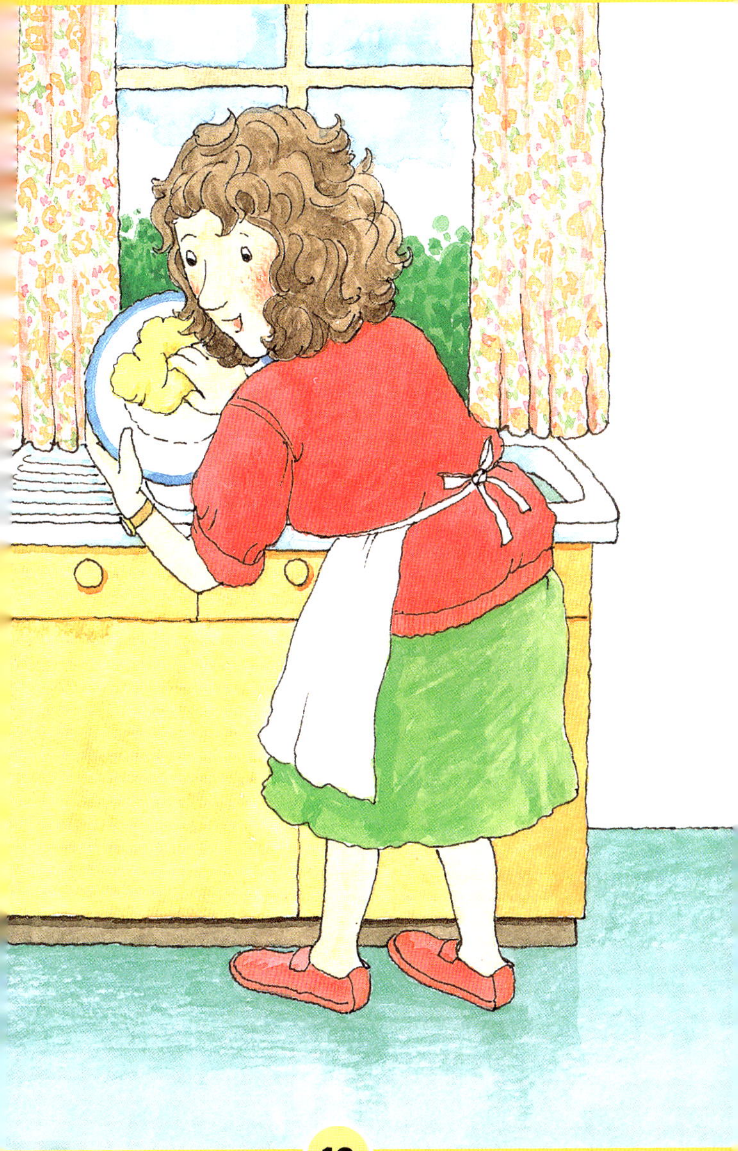

Saffy ran back to the elf.

"Let's paint the tea set," she said. So they did.

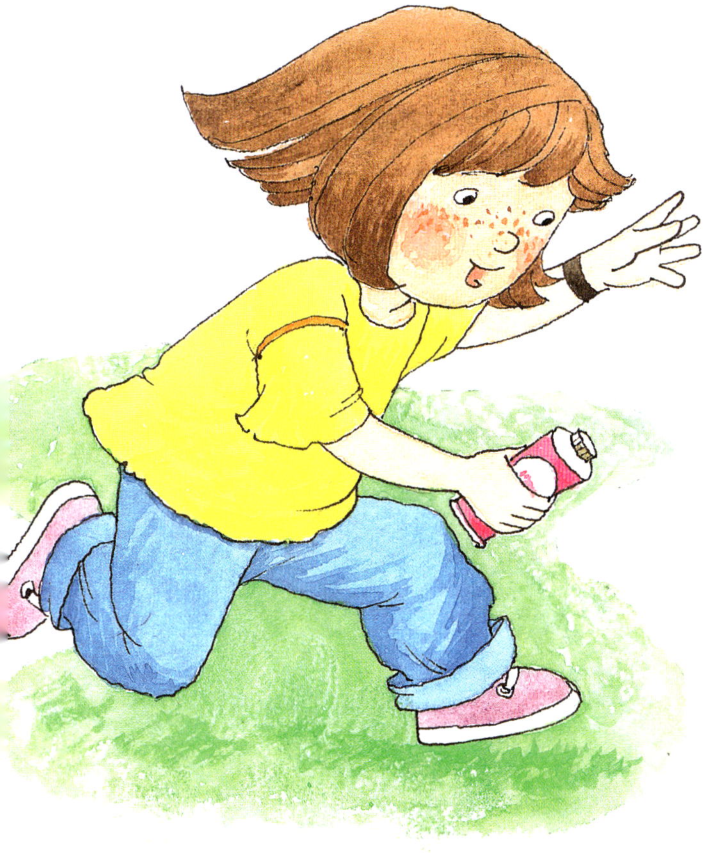

Saffy and the elf had fun with the paint. The elf was in a happy mood now he was not alone.

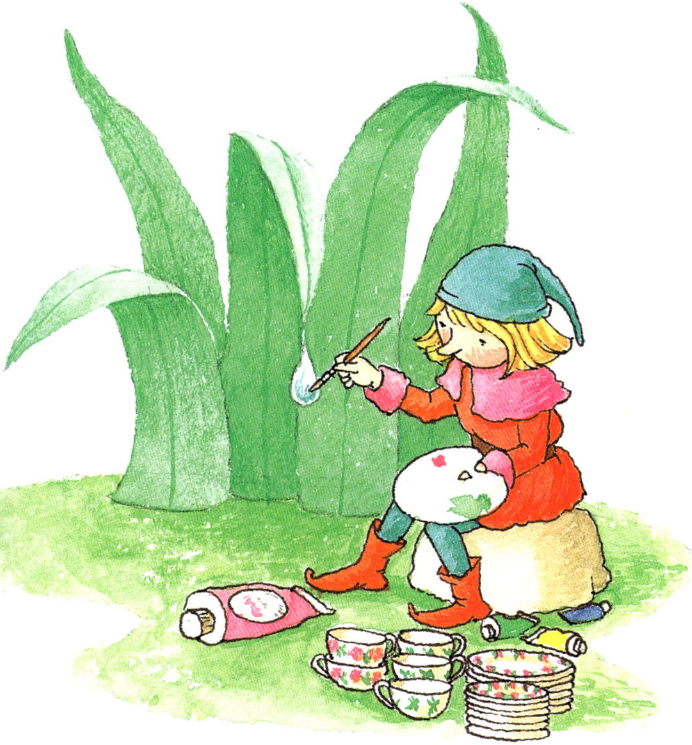

"I will show you some magic," said the elf.

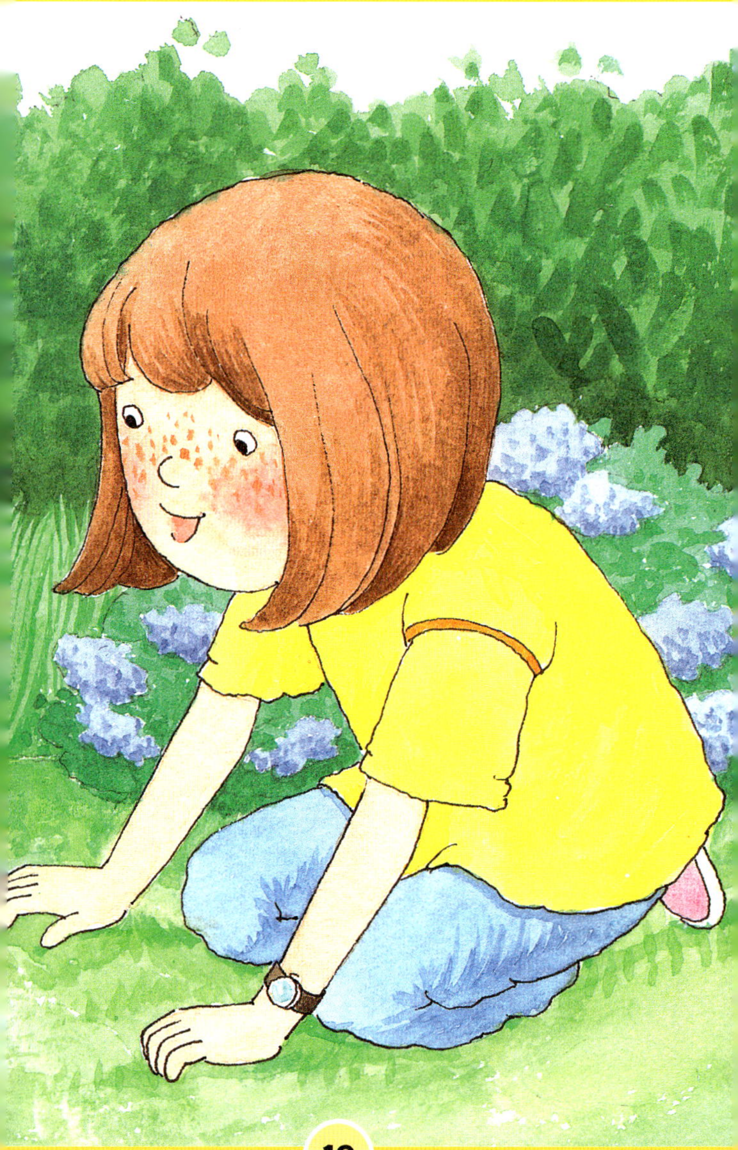

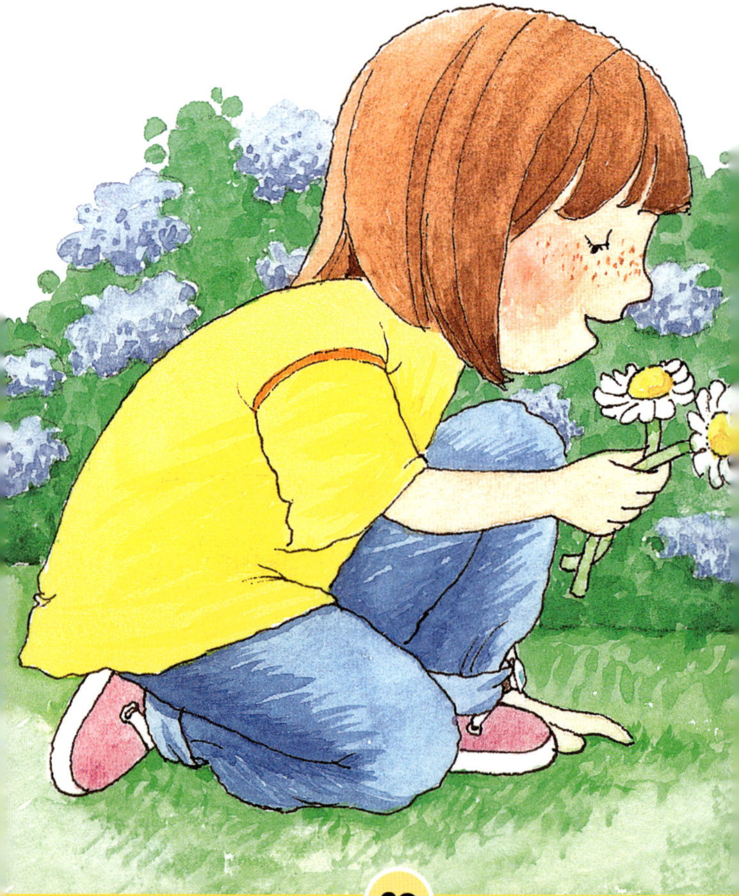

They picked some flowers. Then the elf said some magic words.

22

He made the flowers turn into bees and butterflies.

Saffy and the elf played all day.

"Then Saffy said, "It is tea time. I must go."

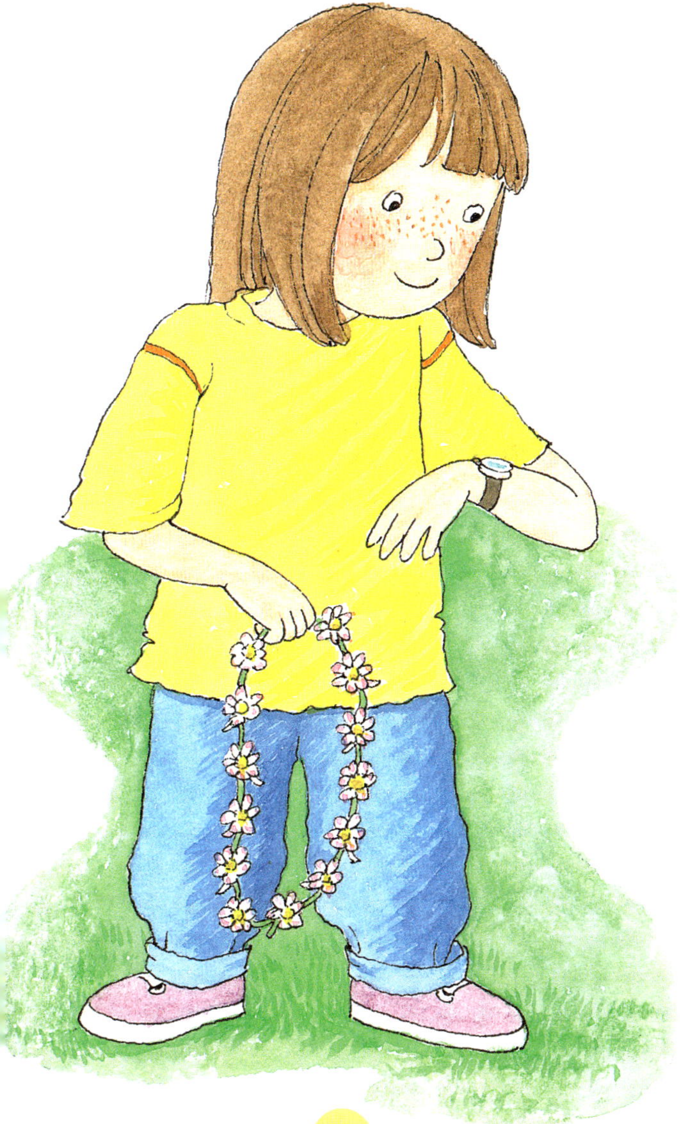

"Let's meet again soon," said the elf.

"Yes! See you soon," said Saffy. "We will be friends forever!"

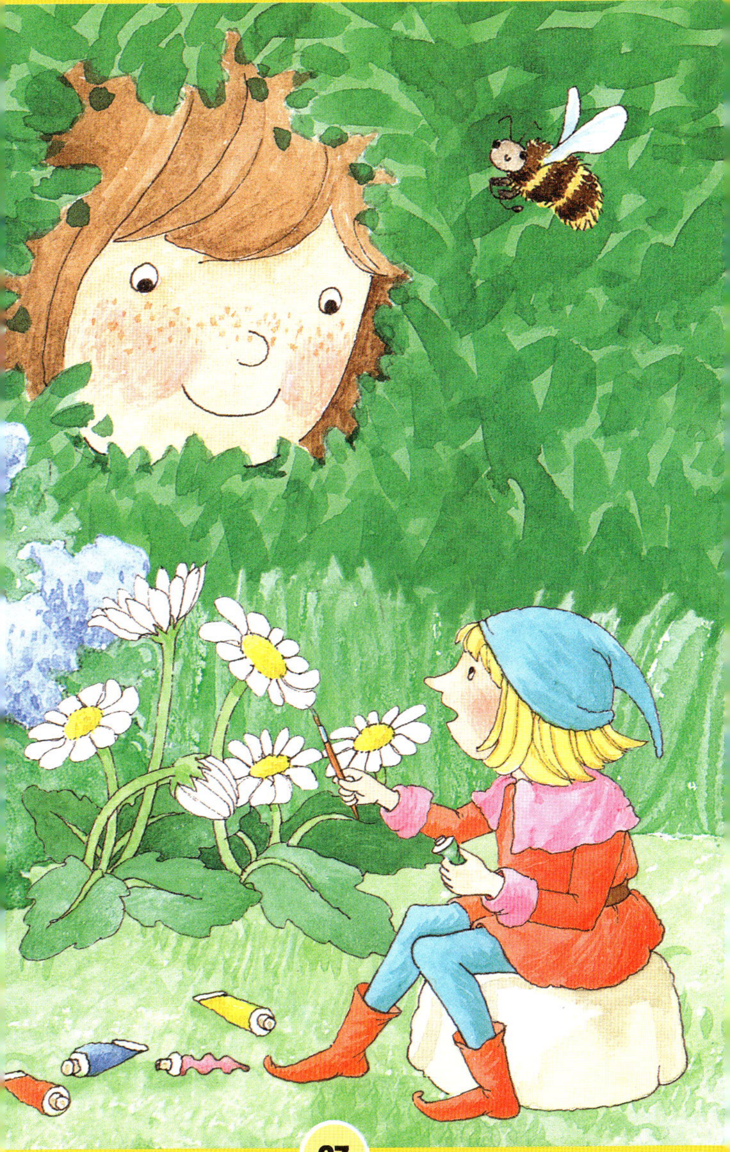

Saffy
Where did Saffy find the elf?

Dad
What do you think Dad would have said to the elf?

bees
How many bees can you find in the book?

elf
Why was the elf sad?

paint
What did Saffy and the elf use the paints for?

flowers
What did the elf do to the flowers?

Notes for Parents and Teachers

Popular Rewards Early Readers have been specially created to build young readers' vocabulary, develop their comprehension skills and boost their progress towards independent reading.

★ Make reading fun. Why not read the story and have your child clap when they hear a featured phonics sound, then race to find it on the page?

★ Encourage your child to read aloud to help pick up and resolve any difficulties. As their skills grow, it will also help their fluency and expression.

★ The list of phonics sounds and 'tough and tricky' words will to help consolidate their learning, and the questions will develop comprehension and communication skills.

★ Always keep a positive attitude and focus on your child's achievements. This will help their confidence and build their enjoyment of reading.

ISBN 978-1-78270-217-7

Illustrated by Colin and Moira Maclean

Copyright © Award Publications Limited
Popular Rewards® is a registered trademark of Award Publications Limited

Published by Award Publications Limited,
The Old Riding School, Welbeck, Worksop, S80 3LR

Printed in Estonia